Jo Weston's

Netball Besties

PENGUIN BOOKS

UK | USA | Canada | Ireland | Australia
India | New Zealand | South Africa | China

Penguin Random House Australia

Penguin Random House Australia is part of the Penguin Random House group of companies whose addresses can be found at global.penguinrandomhouse.com.

First published by Penguin Books, an imprint of Penguin Random House Australia Pty Ltd, in 2025

Cover design by Julie Hally
Internal design by Caroline Lee © Penguin Random House Australia 2025
Cover and internal illustrations by Sam Loman
Author photograph © Grant Treeby

Printed and bound in Australia by Griffin Press, an accredited ISO AS/NZS 14001 Environmental Management Systems printer

NATIONAL LIBRARY OF AUSTRALIA

A catalogue record for this book is available from the National Library of Australia

FSC www.fsc.org MIX Paper | Supporting responsible forestry FSC® C018684

ISBN 978 1 76 134855 6 (Paperback)

Penguin Random House Australia uses papers that are natural and recyclable products, made from wood grown in sustainable forests. The logging and manufacture processes are expected to conform to the environmental regulations of the country of origin.

penguin.com.au

We at Penguin Random House Australia acknowledge that Aboriginal and Torres Strait Islander peoples are the Traditional Custodians and the first storytellers of the lands on which we live and work. We honour Aboriginal and Torres Strait Islander peoples' continuous connection to Country, waters, skies and communities. We celebrate Aboriginal and Torres Strait Islander stories, traditions and living cultures; and we pay our respects to Elders past and present.

Jo Weston's

Netball Besties

Double or Nothing

Written by Jess Black
Illustrated by Sam Loman

PENGUIN BOOKS

CHAPTER ONE

'Almost ready!'

Jo checks her backpack for the third time. Water bottle? *Check.* Purse? *Check.* Netball? *Check.*

'Okay, definitely ready!'

Jo glances at her turquoise suitcase sitting by the door. It's brand new and she's ***excited*** about taking it on her first trip to the city without her family. It's also her first trip to the city to play ***netball***. Lots of firsts!

'I'll miss you!' Jo says to Billie.

Her Australian Shepherd is lying on the mat by the front door, keeping a careful eye on Jo's every move. Billie lets out a soft whine.

Jo gasps. 'Thanks for reminding me, Billie!'

Jo can't believe she almost forgot to pack mini Billie! She runs to her bedroom to grab her ***favourite*** plush toy. There's no way she'll sleep without her furry friend wrapped in her arms, especially when she's so far away from home. She heads back to her suitcase and zips the Billie replica safely inside.

'*Now* I'm ready!' says Jo and gives the real Billie a quick tickle behind the ears. Billie rolls onto her back, inviting Jo to extend the tickle to her tummy.

'Okay, but it has to be quick!' Jo gives Billie's soft belly a rub. 'Don't forget that ***you're in charge*** while I'm away. Look after Mum and Dad!'

'What about us?' Jo's brother James enters the kitchen.

'I figure you and Robert can look after yourselves,' says Jo with a ***grin***. She turns back to Billie. 'And don't let any cheeky cows escape!'

Billie's tail thumps on the floor. Jo hears the crunch of tyres on gravel and peeks out the window to see a white Hilux approaching the house. Ava and her mum are right on time.

'Bye, James!' Jo calls as she swings her backpack over her shoulder and grabs her suitcase. 'See you in a few days!'

Jo's dad is waiting for her at the bottom of the front verandah. He's been out working in their nut orchard since sunrise. 'Good luck for the game. And remember to have fun!'

'I will,' Jo assures him.

Jo's mum is already standing by the car chatting to Ava's mum. When Jo approaches, she gives her a ***squeeze***. 'Love you. Call us when you get there.'

'Will do.' Jo and her suitcase slide into the back seat and soon they're off.

'Morning!' Ava says ***brightly*** to Jo.

'Hi, Ava,' says Jo with an excited giggle.

Billie follows the car as far as the farm gate. As they pull out onto the road, Jo's final image is of her dog watching her go, ears pricked up, tail wagging furiously.

Jo feels a flutter of ***excitement***. She's been to the city before, but not for anything like this. Staying with Ava's family. Playing at half-time in a pro netball game. Exploring all of Ava's favourite old spots. This is going to be a proper adventure!

CHAPTER TWO

The trip to the station feels like it takes *forever*. Luckily, Jo and Ava never run out of things to talk about, so they **happily** sit in the back seat, chatting non-stop.

'I love your suitcase,' Ava says, admiring Jo's compact case and pointing to the red ribbon tied to the handle. 'Ours are just boring black.'

'Thanks.' Jo smiles. 'Mum said it would be a good way to keep track of it – as if the colour isn't bright enough!'

'I can't wait to show you around,' Ava says. 'There's this little bakery near my cousin's house that does the best doughnuts. And there's a laneway full of ***awesome*** murals, and a park where we used to ride our scooters . . .'

Jo laughs. 'How are we supposed to fit all this in *and* play netball?'

Ava's mum glances at them through the rear-view mirror. 'Sounds like you two are going to be very busy.'

'Busy in the best way.' Ava grins. 'There's just so much to show Jo!

I haven't been back to the city since we bought the farm.'

The Country Express train is already waiting on Platform 2 when they arrive. Jo feels a spark of excitement at the sight of the ***gleaming*** silver exterior as she pulls her suitcase along the platform. The wheels roll smoothly, and her case feels light even though she crammed in as much stuff as she could.

Ava's mum glances at the tickets in her hand and nods towards the doors further down the platform. 'We're down here. First Class, Row 7, Seats 3 to 5.'

'Assigned seating.' Jo giggles. 'Fancy!'

'Ooh!' Ava puts on a ***posh accent***. '*And* First Class!'

Both girls are giddy with excitement as they point out every single ***fun*** detail.

'Where do you think they're going?' Jo nods to an elderly couple walking ahead of them.

‘They’re going to the city to see a show to celebrate their 40th wedding anniversary,’ Ava guesses.

‘Aw,’ says Jo.

‘What about those three?’ Ava nods towards what looks like a group of university students.

‘They’re on a field trip for their biology lab,’ says Jo. ‘Ava, do you think people are looking at us and saying that we’re going to play ***netball*** at half-time during a Southern Flames game?’

‘Totally!’ Ava replies. ‘We look like netball pros in our club tracksuits.’

A railway official in a navy uniform checks their tickets. ‘Just through these doors to the left,’ he says.

'You'll see a luggage storage area just inside the doorway for your bigger cases, but you can keep your backpacks with you.'

'Thank you!' both girls call out and then dissolve into more ***giggles***.

The official smiles. 'Have fun, girls.'

'Thanks so much,' says Ava's mum as she steps up onto the train and pulls her case behind her. The girls follow.

It's immediately obvious where they should stash their suitcases. There are already a few lined up in the assigned area by the door. Jo places hers alongside a much larger bright pink case. The girls follow

Ava's mum down the aisle, giving a running commentary.

'Toilets behind us,' says Ava.

'Ooh, and a drinking fountain at the end,' notes Jo.

'No luggage in the aisles,' Ava reads from a notice.

'I'll take the aisle,' says Ava's mum, glancing at the tickets. 'Here we are,' she says, pausing before three empty seats to the right. 'This is us.'

'Jo, you take the window,' says Ava.

'Thanks!' Jo is excited to have the window seat. She can chat to Ava, but it will be ***cool*** to look out of the window and see the changes in scenery. Jo wonders what her mum and dad are up to now. She's been gone for two hours already.

Where is Billie? she thinks. Most likely napping under one of the big walnut trees, or maybe she's helping Dad dig a few holes. Jo feels a pang of ***homesickness***. *Oh, come on,* she tells herself. *You haven't even left Talma Valley yet. Get a grip, Jo!*

'Are you okay?' asks Ava, giving her a curious look.

Jo takes a big breath, then lets out a sigh. She smiles at her friend as she settles into her seat. 'One hundred percent!'

CHAPTER THREE

'These seats are sooo comfy,' Jo says with a sigh. There's a small footrest she can place her feet on, and her ***favourite*** feature is the tray that folds down from the seat in front. She's never flown in a plane, but she imagines it's similar.

'Just think, one day we might be flying to a game,' says Jo excitedly.

Ava nods. 'Melbourne one day, Spain the next!'

Once they're settled in their seats, Ava's mum pulls out a book and begins to read.

The train rumbles to life, but they remain stationary for another few minutes while announcements are made over the intercom.

'Good morning, travellers. Welcome aboard the Country Express service. We will be departing shortly, arriving in Melbourne at approximately 1pm. Orders for our meal service can be placed in our bistro, which is located at the rear of First Class. Thank you for travelling with us, and we hope you enjoy the journey.'

'Meal service!' says Ava, ***jiggling*** about with excitement. 'Let's go check it out!'

'Just wait until we're moving, Ava,' her mum says without glancing up from her book.

'Okay . . .' Ava leans back in her seat with a sigh. 'This is the life, being paid to travel to the city to play netball.'

'We're not being paid!' exclaims Jo.

'No, I know we're not,' says Ava sadly, 'but one day we might.'

Ava ***wiggles*** around to face Jo and leans over her to look out the window.

'Oh my gosh, are you going to be like this the whole trip?' asks Jo.

'What?' asks Ava.

'Completely nuts?' laughs Jo.

'I'm *nut* crazy, Jo.' Ava shakes her head. 'I should have *possibly* mentioned that I find it really hard to sit still for long periods of time. That's why I've brought heaps of things for us to do.'

Ava unzips her backpack and unpacks the contents. She's brought an entire bag of snacks – muesli bars, sour lollies and even some homemade brownies.

'Those look ***amazing***,' Jo says, staring at the brownies.

Ava has also brought activity books, a travel-size chess set, a book and a pair of headphones.

'See, Mum won't let me travel anymore unless I'm super prepared to entertain myself and not annoy her the whole way,' says Ava, placing everything back in her bag.

Ava's mum smiles and pats Ava's leg. 'That's right, Jo. I have learned from years of experience.'

'What have you got in *your* backpack?' Ava asks Jo.

'Ah.' Jo thinks for a split second about what she packed earlier that morning. 'A water bottle, a netball and a map.'

'A map?!' Ava laughs.

'Well, you never know what we might need.'

'It's a terrific idea! I should have thought of that.' Ava spins back around in her seat so she's facing forward again.

The train finally begins to move, and Jo presses her forehead to the glass. It feels **deliciously** cool. The familiar countryside blurs past – rolling paddocks, orchards, clusters of gum trees, the odd mob of sheep munching away.

'It's weird to think we'll be in the city in a couple of hours,' Jo says.

'I know. With traffic lights and proper shops and trams and everything,' Ava says. 'Wait till you see the stadium!'

At the mention of the stadium, Jo is reminded again of the reason for their trip. She still can't quite believe they'll be playing under bright lights in front of thousands of people! It's a ***huge honour*** to be selected to play with other netballers from around the state.

There's a brief silence when Jo thinks Ava might have finally chilled out. Jo settles into the gentle rocking of the train and feels her eyes begin to close. All of a sudden, a hand ***grips*** her knee.

'What is it?' Jo gasps.

'Come on!' says Ava. 'There's no time to waste. We need to check out the bistro!'

'Good luck, Jo.' Ava's mum grins as the girls file past her. 'I have to say, I owe you one!'

Jo grins too as she follows her best friend down the aisle towards the smell of freshly baked pastries and hot chocolate.

CHAPTER FOUR

Jo has eaten her fill of snacks, played three chess games and helped Ava complete a dozen word searches before the city skyline finally comes into view. Jo feels her stomach flip ***excitedly***.

'Such tall buildings,' she says to Ava.

Ava nods.

'And so many houses and apartments,' says Jo.

'Uh-huh,' Ava agrees absentmindedly. Her left leg is ***jiggling*** up and down.

'It's definitely time to get you off this train,' says Jo.

'Heck, yes,' says Ava. 'Hey, let's play some netball when we get to my cousin's house. There's a park just around the corner. Lila and I used to play there all the time. We can go and put your ball to use.'

'Great idea,' agrees Jo. 'And you can burn off some of that pent-up energy at the same time!'

'OMG, we're here!' Ava says.

The train slows as it pulls into the station. Jo watches the people around them gather their things and make their way down the aisles even before the train stops. They're grabbing bags and talking about catching taxis and making dinner reservations. It's ***fun*** to think about what all these people might be going to do as they spill out of the train and make their way into the city.

It's crowded near the train door, but Ava's mum manages to reach over the railing and grab Ava's case. Just then, the doors open and the crowd is suddenly moving. Jo feels herself being caught up among all the passengers. She grabs hold of Ava's hand.

'Wait for me on the platform,' calls Ava's mum from behind them. 'I'll bring your case, Jo.'

Jo lets the surge of the crowd push her forward. It's an uncomfortable feeling and she's relieved when she and Ava are standing on the platform, standing back so other people can move past them.

'***Wow***,' says Jo, 'is it always like that?'

'Welcome to The Big Smoke,' says Ava. 'If you thought *that* was crowded, wait until we get to the stadium!'

Jo feels a ***shiver*** of nerves at the thought. There aren't crowds of people like this back home! It's something she'll have to get used to, here. But then again, the crowd from the train has already scattered. Now there's only a handful of other people left on the platform.

Things sure move fast in the city, Jo thinks.

Ava's mum is also moving fast with all the suitcases and is already marching ahead towards the station exit. Jo and Ava grab their backpacks and ***hurry*** after her.

The main platform is packed with *more* people, all bustling around with suitcases and shopping bags.

Jo stays close to Ava as they weave their way towards the station exit.

'Over here!' a voice calls. 'Yoo-hoo!'

'Aunty *Meeeeeg!*' Ava squeals and waves. She hurries towards a woman with dark hair pulled into a bun, standing by the doors, ***grinning*** and also waving like mad. Beside her is a girl who looks a year or two older than Jo, wearing jeans and a hoodie.

'Aunty Meg! This is Jo,' Ava says as they reach them.

Aunty Meg pulls Ava into a quick hug, then smiles warmly at Jo. 'Lovely to meet you. Welcome to Melbourne.'

JW
JW

The girl next to her gives a ***big smile***. 'Hey, I'm Lila.'

'Hi,' Jo says. 'Thanks for having me.'

'I love having Aves come to stay,' says Lila, looking at Ava with affection. 'And if she's Aves, then you're Country.'

'Some people call me Jo, but hey, you can call me Country if you like,' laughs Jo.

'Come on,' says Aunty Meg. 'Let's get you out of this crowd and home so we can have a cup of tea.'

They all pile into Aunty Meg's car. Ava, Jo and Lila sit in the back with their bags ***squashed*** into the boot. As they pull away from the station, Jo stares out the window.

The streets are so busy – there are cars everywhere, people on bikes and others walking and talking on their phones, rushing around like they've all got somewhere ***important*** to be.

'There's the river,' Ava says, pointing as they cross a wide bridge.

'Wow,' Jo says. 'It's huge.'

'And that's the museum,' Lila adds.

A few blocks later, Ava practically presses her face against the glass. 'Look, Jo. That's the stadium where we're playing!'

'Have you seen the Southern Flames play before, Jo?' asks Aunty Meg.

'Only on TV,' says Jo, her face flushing. 'I can't wait to see a game live!'

Jo leans across the seat for a better view. The stadium is ***massive***, with tall white walls curving like waves and huge banners fluttering out the front.

'Whoa,' Jo breathes. 'That's *enormous*.'

'You should see it at night when it's all lit up,' Lila says. 'It looks amazing.'

Jo feels a flutter of nerves again. Playing at half-time in front of actual crowds in a place like *that*? It suddenly feels very real!

CHAPTER FIVE

'This is us, number 46!' Aunty Meg stops in front of a double-storey terrace house painted in pale yellow. Inside the gate is a small herb and flower garden and a ***glossy*** black door. A large metal doorknocker finishes off the look. It's so different to the large country houses Jo is used to, but she loves it immediately.

Jo can't help but notice how close together everything is in the city. The terrace house looks very narrow and it hardly seems possible that they will all fit inside without being ***squished***. Aunty Meg and Lila live in an older suburb just outside the city. It's a pretty, tree-lined street with row upon row of old terrace houses. Most are white or grey, but some are painted in bright colours, complete with fancy iron fences framing the yards.

'Welcome, Country,' Lila holds the door open for Jo with a flourish.

The inside of the house feels warm and welcoming. The wooden floors creak softly under their feet, and

Jo can smell something sweet like incense or maybe lavender. She follows Ava down a narrow hallway past two bedrooms and into a brightly lit combined kitchen and living area. Jo realises that although the house is narrow, it's actually much larger than it looks from the street. The kitchen table is covered in half-finished ***puzzles*** and bowls of fruit, and a long couch in the living room looks perfect for flopping onto after a big day.

But what really grabs Jo's attention is the style of the house. Each room is painted a different colour and the walls are covered in cool artworks. Some are scenes of horses in paddocks while others are abstract ***splashes*** and marks. Jo can't stop staring.

'Aunty Meg is an interior designer,' Ava explains.

Jo grins. Now it all makes sense. She's never really thought much about how her house looks. Everything is painted white and, apart from the odd netball poster or framed family photograph, her house's walls are kind of bare.

'We're upstairs,' says Ava, signalling Jo to follow her. 'It's pretty cool that we've got our own bathroom as well.'

Jo and Ava drag their bags up the stairs to the room they're sharing.

Jo hears her suitcase go *thud, thud, thud* up each step.

'This is the guest room.' Ava stands aside so that Jo can enter first. Their room is pale green and it feels instantly relaxing. It has two single beds, simple bedside tables with lamps and a colourful rug in the centre.

'This is **so cool**,' Jo says, dropping her suitcase by the bed closest to the window. 'City houses are so . . . different.' The window overlooks the neighbour's narrow backyard, where a ginger cat stretches lazily in a patch of sun.

Ava tosses her backpack onto the other bed.

Jo yawns. The room has made her realise how ***tired*** she is. She hadn't slept much the night before because she'd been so excited about their trip.

'No yawning!' Lila appears in the doorway, bouncing a netball between her hands. 'You two said you wanted to play, right?'

Ava jumps to her feet. 'Absolutely.'

'Let's do it!' Jo adds.

The three girls race down the stairs. Lila grabs a water bottle from the kitchen bench.

'We're off to the park,' says Lila as they head down the hall.

'Be back before dark!' Aunty Meg calls after them.

The park is small but **perfect**. A smooth, open court with faded lines sits right beside a playground where a few younger kids are playing chasey. Lila passes the ball to Jo, who catches it with a solid *thunk*.

'All right,' Lila says, stretching her arms. 'First to five goals wins?'

'You're on,' Ava says.

They start playing, **darting** and **passing**. Jo feels herself slipping into game mode, dodging and weaving as she and Ava try to outplay Lila.

After a particularly tricky shot from Lila, which she sinks easily, Jo bends over to catch her breath. 'Okay,' she pants, 'I admit it. You're good.'

JW

JW

Lila grins. 'Come on, Country, don't give up now.'

Lila taunts Ava and Jo by holding up the ball just out of their reach.

'Nobody said anything about giving up!' Jo cries as she ***leaps*** into the air and grabs the ball from Lila's hands. As they continue to play, Jo feels warm from the game and excited about the next few days. She can't wait to play in the big stadium.

CHAPTER SIX

The smell of something delicious fills the air as Jo, Ava and Lila enter the kitchen. Aunty Meg is stirring a pot on the stove while Ava's mum chops vegetables at the counter. The table has been set and Jo is suddenly ***very hungry***.

'There you are,' Aunty Meg says with a smile. 'How was the park?'

'Lila ***destroyed*** us,' Ava says, dropping into a chair. 'She's been secretly training.'

Lila grins as she refills her water bottle from the tap. 'Not my fault you two need to work on your passing.'

Jo laughs, sliding into a seat. 'We'll be ready for a rematch tomorrow.'

Aunty Meg shakes her head in amusement. 'Well, you'll need your energy for tomorrow's big game, so eat up.' She carries a dish of steaming pasta to the table while Ava's mum brings over a salad.

As they dig in, Aunty Meg turns to Jo. 'So, first time in the city for a netball trip?'

Jo nods, twirling pasta around her fork. 'We've visited the city but usually to see family, or if Dad needs to come on farm business. Oh! That reminds me, I've brought some nuts for you from the farm. They're in my case.'

'Thank you, Jo,' Aunty Meg ***beams***. She nods towards Ava's mum. 'I have to admit, I've been buying Talma Valley Nuts since Claire told me about you, so I'm thrilled to have more!'

'And you're both playing in the same team now, is that right?' she asks Ava.

Ava nods. 'The Junior Wildcats.'

'Our netball courts at home feel tiny compared to the stadium,' says Jo.

'You'll love it,' Aunty Meg says. 'Nothing like playing in front of a ***big crowd***.'

Lila perks up. 'Speaking of netball, we're meeting the other girls in your team in the morning for a training session. Coach Bree wants us to have a run-through before the match.'

Ava groans. 'I was hoping for a sleep-in.'

'You know Coach,' Lila says. 'She's all about preparation.' She turns to Jo. 'It'll be a good chance for you to meet everyone before the game. I've heard there are girls who've come from even further away than you.'

'Lila was selected a few years ago and now she helps out,' Ava explains.

'You're following in my footsteps, Aves!' Lila teases. Ava rolls her eyes.

Jo's nerves are flickering again. She hopes she fits in with the rest of their team. Jo and Ava were specially selected for this **opportunity** after a scout picked them out at a Wildcats club game in Talma Valley. If Lila is only helping out she probably won't be with them the whole time, so Ava will be the only person Jo will know at training tomorrow.

After dinner, the girls help clear the table before heading upstairs to get ready for bed.

‘Is it okay if I have a shower?’ asks Jo. ‘I’m a bit sweaty after that game.’

‘Absolutely,’ says Ava. ‘I think the towels are in the bathroom.’

Jo grabs her suitcase and notices something ***strange***: the red ribbon that was tied to the handle is gone. *Maybe it fell off at the train station or in the car*, Jo thinks. She shrugs and flips it open so she can grab her pyjamas.

She frowns. Inside her suitcase sits a pair of sparkly high-top sneakers, a blue hoodie and a toiletry bag she’s never seen before.

Her heart gives a ***little skip***.

Jo stares at the open case and the unfamiliar contents that seem to have replaced her stuff. She blinks once. Twice.

'This . . . isn't my bag,' she says, her voice flat.

Ava glances over. 'What do you mean? It looks like yours.'

Jo shakes her head, flipping through things that aren't hers.

'I thought it was . . . but mini Billie's not here.'

She runs her hands over the suitcase's contents again, as if her favourite plush toy might be hiding underneath. But no.

She closes the case, her stomach twisting. Jumbled thoughts race through Jo's mind. She has no idea how this could have happened, but she feels an instant ***pang*** for her own clothes, shoes and, most importantly, mini Billie.

'This is definitely not my suitcase,' she states firmly.

Ava's eyes widen. 'Wait. If this isn't yours . . . then whose is it? Do you think someone switched them by accident? Or on purpose?'

'I don't know.' Jo swallows hard. 'But I need to find my suitcase.'

Ava's mum frowns as she listens to the recorded message. *'We're sorry, but the lost property office is currently unattended . . .'*

She sighs and leaves a message after the beep explaining what has happened and asking for someone to call her if Jo's suitcase is handed in. When she hangs up, she turns back to the girls, who are watching **anxiously**.

'Well,' Ava's mum says, 'I could only leave a voicemail. It *is* after hours.'

'We'll check back with them first thing in the morning,' Aunty Meg adds, trying to sound ***cheerful***. 'Right now, though, you two need to get some sleep. Jo, I'm sure we can find you some pyjamas to wear.'

Jo nods, but her stomach twists. What if they don't? What if her bag is halfway to some other part of the city by now? Her suitcase is full of important gear for the game – her court shoes, the special pass she needs to enter the stadium and worst of all . . .

What about mini Billie?

CHAPTER SEVEN

'Rise and shine, sleepyhead!'

Jo is ***startled awake*** to find Ava standing over her.

Ava gives her shoulder a playful squeeze. 'We need to get to training.'

It takes a beat for Jo to realise that she's not at home on the farm, but in Ava's cousin's house in the city. She's had a ***terrible*** sleep. In one dream, her suitcase was running down the platform into a dark tunnel and, no matter how fast she ran, she couldn't catch it. The other dream was worse. It involved mini Billie, alone on a dark street corner. Jo ***shudders*** at the memory. And all of this with no mini Billie to cuddle.

'What's the time?' Jo asks.

'It's after nine o'clock,' says Ava who is, Jo sees, already dressed in her netball kit. 'You were dead to the world, so we decided it was better to let you sleep in.'

'Thanks,' says Jo as she jumps out of bed.

'We're leaving in fifteen,' says Ava. 'I've got Vegemite toast for you to eat in the car.'

'Yum!'

Jo blinks. She'd almost forgotten. 'Oh no . . . my kit's in my suitcase.'

'It's okay,' Ava says, ***rummaging*** through her case. 'You can borrow my spare stuff. I brought two of everything. Lucky you wore your club tracksuit!'

Jo quickly changes into Ava's extra set of training clothes. The shirt is fine, but the shorts are . . . snug.

'Sorry,' Ava says, cringing as Jo tugs at the waistband.

Jo tries to twist and bend in them, but they feel like they're clinging in all the wrong places.

'It's fine,' Jo says, even though it's definitely *not* fine. 'I'll survive.'

Lila knocks on the door, holding out a pair of sneakers.

'Here, you can borrow these,' she says.

Jo slips them on and immediately feels her toes **squished** up at the top of the shoe. She wiggles them. Then wiggles them again.

'They're . . . perfect,' Jo lies.

'They're probably a bit small,' Lila says, frowning.

'Just a bit,' Jo admits, standing up and feeling like a stuffed sausage.

Ava winces. 'Not the best start, hey?'

Jo gives a lopsided smile. 'Nope. But what matters is that we're here and we're playing.'

'That's the spirit!' Ava jokes.

They both laugh, but Jo can't help feeling a bit off. She's been ***looking forward*** to this trip for weeks, and now here she is in clothes that don't fit, shoes that pinch and no sign of her suitcase anywhere. It just doesn't make any sense.

'Has your mum heard back from the lost property office?' she asks.

Ava shakes her head. 'No, and she's called twice.'

Jo sighs. There is nothing for it but to head out the door.

'Maybe things will feel better once we're on court,' Jo says, trying to shake the nerves.

'Definitely,' Ava agrees. 'Let's go ***smash*** it at training. Bad clothes, bad shoes – but great ball skills.'

Jo nods and follows her down the stairs, wincing as she goes, hoping Ava is right.

CHAPTER EIGHT

'Whoa!'

Jo tilts her head back as they walk towards the entrance of the netball stadium. It looks even bigger up close. She takes in the huge stands and rows of glass windows reflecting the afternoon sky.

'This place is ***wild***,' Jo says quietly.

Ava nods. 'Told you.'

Inside, they check in at the front desk and are directed to one of the side courts for training. Jo can already hear the squeak of trainers on polished floors and the echo of balls ***thudding*** against the rings. Jo tries to quell her nerves, but this place feels like a lot.

'This is where Coach said to bring you,' says Lila.

A few girls are already gathered at their court, standing around in small groups, fiddling with water bottles or tying up shoelaces. No one really seems to be talking.

Jo and Ava glance at each other.

'Guess we just . . . go over?' Ava says.

'Yep.'

Jo tugs at the waistband of the too-tight shorts and follows Ava across the court.

'Hi,' Ava says brightly to the group.

A tall girl with her hair in a perfect plait looks them up and down but doesn't greet them. A couple of the girls ***mumble*** quiet hellos. Jo realises that everyone is as nervous as she is and it makes her feel a little better.

'Hi, everyone!' A woman in a blue tracksuit and hair in a messy bun approaches. Her smile is bright and warm, and she walks with a spring in her step. She's wearing the telltale whistle on a lanyard around her neck.

'I'm Coach Bree. Gather around. I know some of you have travelled a long way to be here, so first up – amazing effort just making the team. You should be really ***proud*** to have been selected. It's an honour to play at half-time and also lots of fun!'

Jo feels herself relax a tiny bit. Coach Bree is full of positive energy, which helps counter the nerves. She can see the other girls also relaxing as they listen to her talk.

'Okay, let's get moving,' Coach Bree says. 'We'll start with a warm-up and some passing drills. Don't worry about not having played together before. That's what this morning is all about.'

They jog laps first, and Jo immediately regrets the too-tight shorts and the tiny shoes. The waistband digs in, and her toes pinch with every step. She can feel the beginnings of blisters on both big toes.

'You good?' Ava whispers as they pass each other.

'Totally fine,' Jo replies. There's no way she's going to let her discomfort ruin Ava's experience.

Next are passing drills. It starts okay, but then the ***nerves*** creep in. Passes go wide. The ball fumbles through fingers. No one's quite sure who's next, and the circle starts to fall apart.

'Call for it!' Coach Bree encourages. 'Don't be shy!'

But everyone *is* shy.

No one speaks much except for Perfect Plait Girl, who seems very happy to tell people where they're supposed to stand and who should be doing what.

'Maybe throw it *a bit* earlier next time,' she says pointedly to Jo after a missed pass.

Jo gives a tight smile. 'Sure.'

Then they split into teams for a short practice game. Jo and Ava end up on opposite sides, and Jo's team struggles from the get-go. People ***hesitate*** before passing. Nobody seems sure where to run.

Jo tries to intercept, but the borrowed sneakers are stiff and she can't get the grip she wants.

The game finishes with a pretty sad scoreline, but Coach Bree claps her hands together and beams.

'Awesome work, everyone! I know it feels ***a bit messy***, but that's totally normal. You're still learning each other's styles. Trust me, we're going to pull this together beautifully.'

Jo stands up a bit straighter and forces a smile. She appreciates the optimism, but she can't help thinking, *We're going to need a miracle before half-time tonight!*

She and Ava meet by the bench to grab their water bottles.

'Well,' Ava says, wiping sweat from her forehead. 'That was . . . a start.'

'A very wobbly start,' Jo agrees. 'But hey, at least no one broke a finger.'

They both laugh, but Jo can't help **worrying**.

The stadium. The crowd. And this team that can barely manage a smooth pass?

It's starting to feel like the real challenge of the weekend might not be finding her missing suitcase.

It might be surviving the game.

CHAPTER NINE

Jo tries to shake off her anxiety about the game once they are back at Lila's house, but she can't stop thinking about the ***missing suitcase***. Or rather, *her* suitcase. The one that isn't currently in her possession.

Ava's mum hangs up the phone for the fifth time. 'Still no real person on the lost property hotline,' she sighs. 'Just another recording. I'm sorry, Jo. I don't know what else to suggest.'

Jo slumps back in her seat. 'It's just so frustrating.'

'Maybe we need to work backwards,' says Ava. 'Figure out who *owns* the case you have.'

Jo sits upright. 'Yes! Find the person, find my suitcase! Ava, you're a ***genius***.'

'I've been saying that for years.' Ava grins. 'It's about time someone listened!'

'Have you looked inside?' asks Aunty Meg.

Jo shakes her head. 'Just enough to know it's not mine.'

'If it helps us return it, I think it's okay – as long as you're respectful,' Ava's mum says gently.

Ava doesn't need more ***encouragement***. She's halfway to the stairs before anyone can blink. Lila jumps out of the way as Ava bolts past.

'Wait for me!' Jo calls, scrambling after her.

The old stairs groan under their feet as they thunder upstairs.

'Careful, elephants!' Aunt Meg calls after them. 'This house is older than all of us combined.'

'Sorry!' Ava yells back, laughing.

They reach the green room, puffing.

'Hang on,' Jo says, ripping off Lila's shoes. She grins as she spreads her toes out. 'That's better.'

'Focus, detective,' says Ava.

They kneel on the colourful rug in front of the suitcase. Jo flips open the lid.

First out: the ***glittery*** high-tops. Then, the plain blue hoodie. No logo, no name.

'What if we find treasure?' asks Ava. 'Can we split it fifty-fifty?'

'Unlikely,' laughs Jo. 'We're more likely to find skincare products and undies!'

'Boring!' says Ava.

'Okay, what's next?' Jo mutters as she pulls out the nightie and other clothes. She then spots a navy polo shirt at the bottom. 'There's a logo,' she says, smoothing the fabric.

Ava leans in. 'That looks like a netball club.'

Lila appears in the doorway, arms folded. 'Stormers. Solid team. A girl from my school played for them once.'

'***Bingo***,' Ava whispers. 'We have something. Somewhere to start.'

'Except, that club disbanded a few years ago,' said Lila.

Ava gives her a look.

Jo keeps digging – track pants, a water bottle and a battered leather notebook. She flips it open: pages filled with drills, training plans and a few dates circled in red.

'Whoever this is, they're serious about ***netball***,' Jo says quietly.

'Check the front page,' Ava says, peering over her shoulder. 'Maybe there's a name?'

Jo turns to the first page. Nothing. Just more tidy handwriting.

'A coach, maybe?' Ava wonders.

Jo shrugs. She sets the notebook aside and lifts out a few smaller items: a charger, some keys with a Tower of London keyring, hand cream and a paperback novel. She opens it to find a train ticket tucked inside.

'She was on our train,' Jo confirms. 'She got on at . . . Benalla.'

Lila raises an eyebrow. 'Country player. Visiting the city?'

'Just like us.' Jo nods slowly.

She zips open the inside pocket – and freezes.

'What is it?' asks Ava.

Jo lifts out a small velvet box. The kind you don't just stumble across.

Lila and Ava gather around Jo as she cracks it open.

Inside, nestled in soft black velvet, is a Commonwealth Games gold medal. The ribbon reads *Manchester 2002.*

Jo stares. Her throat goes dry.

Ava gasps. '***Whoa***.'

'No way,' Lila breathes. 'That's the *real* deal.'

Jo's mind spins as she stares at the gleaming medal. Whoever this suitcase belongs to . . . she's not just a netballer.

She's a champion.

CHAPTER TEN

Everyone stares in silence at the gold medal in the centre of the kitchen table, nestled in its black velvet box.

'I can't believe it's a ***real gold medal***,' says Jo.

'They're not made of pure gold,' explains Aunty Meg. 'It's sterling silver with gold plating. Still, it's very impressive. I've never seen one up close before.'

'It's so much heavier than I thought it would be,' says Lila, picking up the medal by the ribbon and letting it ***dangle*** gently. 'I mean, feel the weight on this thing.'

'Assuming the medal belongs to the owner of the suitcase, it certainly narrows down who that owner might be,' says Ava.

'A gold medal winner,' says Jo, nodding.

'I've already looked it up online,' says Ava's mum. 'Australia won gold at Manchester in 2002. Apparently, it was an ***epic*** game.' She reads from her phone. 'The Diamonds won the gold medal after a thrilling double extra-time final against New Zealand, with a final score of 57–55. There were eighteen players in the squad.'

'Hmm, that doesn't feel like it's narrowed the field all that much,' says Ava.

'We know the owner of the case is visiting the city like us,' says Jo. 'And we know they like netball.'

'Maybe they're here for a special occasion?' suggests Aunty Meg.

'Like visiting family?' says Ava.

'There could be a million reasons why they're here, we just need to find out where they are,' says Jo. 'And hope they're sitting here like us, looking at *my* suitcase, trying to figure out who *I* am.'

Ava ***leaps*** out of her chair clicking her fingers.

'Do you think the stuff in your suitcase has clues to who you are?' asks Ava.

Jo thinks for a minute. 'I'm not sure what this says about me, but my suitcase is full of bags of nuts, my netball kit, pyjamas and mini Billie. Oh, and a hairbrush.'

'They're unlikely to think you live on a nut farm, just because you've got a few bags of nuts in your suitcase,' says Aunty Meg.

'Just that you're a *nut* case,' jokes Ava.

Jo shoots her a ***withering*** look – *ha ha.*

'I'll call the netball federation and leave word that we have this case with its valuable contents. That's really all we can do for now,' says Aunty Meg.

'So much for solving the ***mystery***,' Jo says with a sigh. She's dreading putting Lila's sneakers back on. She was so looking forward to this game and now she just wants to get it all over with as fast as possible.

'We've got a bit of time before you need to be at the stadium,' says Aunty Meg ***brightly***, clearly trying to lift Jo's spirits. 'Why don't we do a little sightseeing?'

Ava nods enthusiastically. Jo looks up.

'Are you talking about museums and things?' she asks cautiously.

Ava's mum laughs. 'I'm not talking about anything. It's up to you girls.'

'Whatever we do, I'm not letting this suitcase out of my sight,' says Jo.

'We'll take you wherever you want to go, Jo,' says Aunty Meg. 'You don't get to come to the city very often. What would you most like to do?'

Jo and Ava make eye contact and Jo grins.

'Are you thinking what I'm thinking?' Ava asks Jo.

Jo ***squeals***, then smiles. 'Let's go nuts!'

CHAPTER ELEVEN

Jo is still squealing as they step through the entrance of the fun park. All her worries about her suitcase and her crowded toes have ***vanished*** – she is now back in her comfy club tracksuit and her own shoes – and been replaced by the thrill of going on a roller-coaster. Bright banners flap overhead, music pulses from hidden speakers, and the smell of hot chips and popcorn hits them like a wall.

'I've always wanted to go to a fun park!' Jo cries. 'The annual circus that comes to Talma Valley does *not* cut it.'

She spins in a slow circle to take it all in. 'This place is ***awesome***.'

'Let's split up for a bit,' says Aunty Meg. 'We'll meet you back by the car in about an hour. That gives you time for a few rides and a snack before we head to the stadium.'

'Can we go on whatever we want?' Jo asks, bouncing slightly on the balls of her feet.

'As long as you stick together,' says Ava's mum. 'Would you like me to keep the suitcase?'

'No, thank you,' says Jo firmly, holding onto the turquoise ***imposter***. 'This baby is staying with me.'

'Got it,' laughs Ava's mum.

'Go have fun!' Aunty Meg waves them off.

The moment they're alone, the girls burst into motion, Jo dragging the suitcase behind her like a very clunky, awkward handbag. It bumps along the cobbled path as they weave past balloon vendors and a man on stilts juggling bowling pins.

Music spills from the carousel, and kids run around holding ***bright*** slushies and oversized soft toys with googly eyes that dart in every direction.

'This place is incredible,' Jo says, wide-eyed. 'Where do we even start?'

They start with the Laughing Clowns. Jo is determined to beat them, leaning into each ball toss like a total athlete, her tongue poking out the side of her mouth in ***concentration***. She gets two clowns in a row, but the third just wobbles annoyingly.

'These games are rigged,' Ava mutters as she lines up for her turn.

After that is the ring-toss game, where Jo wins an inflatable hammer that ***squeaks*** every time she smacks Ava on the arm. Ava then scores a fluoro green lizard keyring. They're breathless when they stumble into the next area, where the roar of the roller-coaster echoes like thunder.

'That looks insane,' Jo says, pointing up at the towering wooden frame.

'We are definitely doing that,' Ava replies with a grin.

They're halfway up the line when they hear someone call out. It's Lila, waving from a bench nearby with a giant swirl of ***fairy floss*** in her other hand.

'Hey, ***legends***! You two going on that thing?'

'Yeah! Come with us?!' Jo yells back.

Lila shakes her head. 'No way. I like my brain where it is. I'll mind the case, Country.'

Jo glances at the suitcase at her feet. 'Thanks! That'd be awesome.'

They pass the suitcase over the barrier to Lila.

'Good thing you came along,' says Jo.

'Guard it with your life,' Ava says, mock serious.

'Yeah, yeah,' Lila replies.

'I mean it!' says Ava.

'I'm older and therefore much more responsible than either of you.' Lila ***salutes*** with her fairy floss. 'I will *not* let this suitcase out of my sight!'

CHAPTER TWELVE

The roller-coaster clanks and rattles as it begins its slow, suspenseful ascent. Jo ***buzzes*** with excitement, but her knuckles are white where she grips the safety bar.

'I can't believe we're doing this!' she laughs, eyes wide as the track rises in front of them like a jagged steel mountain.

'No going back now!' Ava shouts, grinning in a *this might have been a mistake but it's too late to do anything about it* way.

Their car climbs higher and higher. The fairground shrinks beneath them.

'Look at how tiny everything looks,' says Jo, taking in

the little candy-coloured stalls and ant-sized people. Wind whips at their hair. Jo peers down the side of their car and immediately regrets it. As their carriage ***creeps*** to the summit, time seems to slow down.

Jo leans towards Ava, voice pitched with panic. 'Do you think we'll throw up or cry first?'

'Definitely cry,' Ava yells – and, just like that, gravity disappears and Jo's stomach ***plummets***.

The drop hits like a punch to the gut, and then the world becomes a blur. *AAAAHHHHHHHHHH!*

Jo's scream is lost to the air above. Her eyes are jammed closed and the wind slaps her face. The roller-coaster jerks hard left, then plunges into a tunnel so black that it swallows the light.

Inside the tunnel, everything changes. No lights, no sense of direction. Just sound and speed. Ava's laugh cuts into a ***shriek*** as the roller-coaster spins into a tight corkscrew. Jo can't tell if her eyes are open or closed – either way, she can't see.

'This is crazy!' Jo screams. She touches her cheeks but can no longer feel her face.

Ava is laughing hysterically, or maybe she's crying. Jo can't tell.

Jo's arms fly up as the roller-coaster surges out of the tunnel and straight into a loop. Her scream turns into manic laughter.

Every twist is faster, sharper than the last. A near miss with a low beam. A sudden bank so ***sharp*** Jo nearly slams into Ava's shoulder. The track dips again, then launches upward into one final surge.

Then, all of a sudden, it's over and Jo is falling back into her seat as the roller-coaster brakes. It creeps calmly into the platform, as if everything that just happened was a dream. Silence, then a collective ***exhale*** from everyone on board.

Jo and Ava stagger out, legs like jelly. Their hair is sticking out at wild angles, their faces red from the wind and screaming.

'Best ride *ever*,' Jo pants, half-laughing.

They stumble back towards the bench where they left Lila, still buzzing and dizzy.

'Lila's not going to believe how fast that thing was . . .'

Ava stops.

Jo blinks. 'What?'

The bench is still there. So is the half-eaten fairy floss, its stick lying across the wrapper like it was just set down.

But Lila is gone.

And so is the suitcase.

CHAPTER THIRTEEN

'That's weird,' says Ava. 'Lila wouldn't just leave perfectly good fairy floss uneaten. Not to mention, Lila would never litter.'

The girls spin in opposite directions, scanning the crowd. Jo still feels shaky from the ride. Her centre of gravity has shifted and the grounded world feels alien.

'Hang on, look!' Jo points towards the dodgem cars. Weaving between a group of kids eating ***tornado potatoes*** on sticks is a flash of strawberry-blonde hair.

'Why's she running away from us?' asks Ava.

'Lila!' Jo shouts, already breaking into a jog. 'Hey!'

But Lila doesn't stop.

As fast as their wobbly limbs can carry them, Ava and Jo hurry after Lila. A man in a koala costume jumps back as they fly past. 'Whoa! Careful!'

'She's chasing something.' Jo ducks under a long string carrying a neon pink balloon. 'Look!'

Up ahead, a small electric buggy zips along the main path. Jo suddenly realises why Lila is running after it – on the back of the buggy is the turquoise suitcase! It's wedged between a crate of stage lights and what appears to be a ***feather boa***.

'Stop!' cries Jo. 'That's our suitcase!'

Jo feels nauseous. It's mainly from the roller-coaster, but she also feels sick at the thought of losing *another* suitcase. This one isn't even hers, but it's the closest thing she's got to getting hers back.

'Lila, wait!' calls Ava, out of breath.

They push harder, feet slapping pavement, hearts pounding. Music blares from a nearby ride. Bubbles float randomly through the air.

Jo and Ava finally catch up to Lila near the funhouse entrance. She's bent over, hands on her knees, ***gasping***.

'It was *right* next to me,' she huffs. 'I looked up at you two on the roller-coaster for about three seconds – then it was *gone*! I thought maybe it rolled off, but then suddenly it was driving away.'

'It's okay,' Jo says, scanning for the buggy. 'Where'd it go?'

'That way!' Lila jabs a finger toward a narrow path.

They're off again and, this time, they're closing in. Jo can see the back of the driver's head. A man with black hair pulled back in a loose ponytail. The buggy turns a corner up ahead and slows down to enter a narrow laneway lined with vendors.

'Stop!' calls Jo.

'You've got our suitc–' Ava doubles over, completely out of breath.

For a beat, they just stand there, breathing hard, sweat cooling on their backs.

After giving Ava a second, the girls keep running, but the laneway is filled with people and they have to ***dodge*** the crowd.

'It's up ahead!' cries Lila.

'He's taking the suitcase out of the buggy!' cries Ava.

Sure enough, the driver disappears and re-emerges emptyhanded.

'Who would want to ***steal*** a suitcase?' asks Jo, feeling completely frustrated.

'Maybe they thought the suitcase was part of a costume drop-off or something?' Ava suggests.

'There *was* a feather boa back there,' Lila agrees.

'Well, I'm not giving up,' says Jo.

By the time they reach the spot where the buggy was parked, the suitcase and the driver are long gone.

JW

A brightly painted trailer sits slightly apart from the other vendors. The name 'Seraphina' is painted in bright yellow. The door is open but strands of colourful beads cover the entry.

'Look,' Lila says, gesturing past the beaded curtain.

Jo's eyes immediately spot what Lila is pointing at: a turquoise suitcase.

CHAPTER FOURTEEN

'Come inside, girls,' says a voice from inside the trailer.

The girls share a look and Jo makes a decision. 'After you, Lila.'

'My pleasure,' she says as she lifts the beaded curtain. The strands clink together with a soft, ***unsettling*** chime.

'This is so creepy,' Ava whispers to Jo as she steps inside.

'*Shhh*,' Jo whispers back.

A woman sits behind a table, her face lit from below. She wears black from head to toe – layers of lace and silk – and her long dark hair frames eyes rimmed in heavy, ***dramatic*** make-up.

'Welcome, girls,' she says, her voice deep and smooth. 'I've been expecting you.'

The air around them is thick with the smell of incense. The room is dim, lit only by the soft, pulsing glow of a crystal ball resting on the velvet-draped table. Jo sees something on the floor beside the woman.

She steps forward. 'I think you have our suitcase.'

The woman's eyes glint. 'Yes. Samuel thought it was mine. They are very similar, are they not?' She gestures to the corner of the room where they can see an older, scuffed turquoise suitcase that is almost identical to Jo's.

Jo leans closer and ***squints***. 'You're right!'

'Just how many people own this exact brand and colour of suitcase?' exclaims an exasperated Lila.

The woman tilts her head, suddenly very still. 'But . . . am I also right in thinking this case does not actually belong to you?'

The woman's gaze is intense, like she's looking into Jo's soul. It's a very ***strange*** feeling.

'How did you know that?' Jo asks.

'Like I said before,' says Ava quietly. 'Creepy . . .'

The woman's red lips curl into a small smile. 'The great Seraphina cannot reveal her sources.'

'Have you been spying on us?' Lila asks with an accusatory tone.

'Let's just say . . . I have a gift.'

Seraphina gestures toward the chairs around the table. 'Please. Sit.'

The girls exchange a look.

'Should we?' Ava murmurs.

'What have we got to lose?' says Jo, pulling out a chair.

Jo and Ava sit. Lila remains standing by the doorway, arms crossed.

Seraphina closes her eyes for a beat, then opens them slowly. 'I sense you're here because you have a question for me.'

'We do?' Lila asks, brows raised.

'Can you tell us who this suitcase belongs to?' Jo says quickly.

Seraphina smiles a knowing smile, as if this scene has already played out in her mind. She places her hands on either side of the glowing orb and closes her eyes again. Her lips begin to move – low, ***rhythmic*** whispers in a language none of them recognise. Not quite words, more like echoes of something old.

Her fingers hover just above the crystal ball, her eyelids ***fluttering*** like she's dreaming with her eyes. Jo shares a look with Ava. This all feels very staged but, the way Jo sees it,

they have nothing to lose by seeing it through.

'She is near,' she murmurs. 'The one you seek.'

The ball's glow pulses faintly, the shadows deepening around them.

'She sits with others. Women bound by victory . . . and time.'

Jo glances at Ava.

Ava mouths, *What does that mean?*

Seraphina's voice drops lower.

'You'll find her . . . where bells once rang. And time is of the essence.' Her eyes flick open. 'Look out for the red doors.'

Ava leans forward, her voice **sharp**. 'Where is this?'

But Seraphina only smiles. 'The path will show itself. If you're paying attention.'

A long, ***charged*** silence follows.

Then Jo stands. 'Come on. We'll figure it out.' She hands Seraphina the inflatable hammer she won earlier and takes back the suitcase. 'Thanks.'

As Jo turns her back, she can feel Seraphina's gaze boring into the back of her head.

They step back out into the sunshine. The fresh air is a ***welcome*** change after being inside the trailer.

'What a load of rubbish,' says Lila, glancing back through the curtain.

'Careful,' says Ava. 'She might put a curse on you.'

Lila rolls her eyes.

'Bells ringing, red doors . . . what about a fire station?' says Jo.

'There's a big one not far from here!' says Ava, catching on. 'It's got red doors!'

'You're right,' says Lila reluctantly.

Behind them, the beaded curtain stills. And the ***strangeness*** of the room slips away to be replaced by the reassuring sounds of fun-park crowds.

CHAPTER FIFTEEN

Lila fires off a text to the mums updating them that they'll still be on time to meet up but are checking out a fire station two blocks away.

Aunty Meg: *Uh . . . why?*

Lila: *Tell you when we see you.*

Ava isn't wrong. There is a historic fire station only two blocks away from the fun park. The girls pull up out the front.

'Thank goodness for your map,' Ava says to Jo as they compare the street names in front of them with those on the ***map***.

'This has to be it,' says Lila, panting.

It's a sturdy brick building with arched red doors and tall windows, the kind that looks like it's been standing forever. A faded gold sign across the top reads, *City Fire Station – 1894*.

'I've never been inside a fire station before,' says Jo, taking a minute to catch her breath.

'Neither have I,' says Ava.

'That makes three of us!' says Lila. 'Although I have ridden in a fire truck once. That was pretty cool.'

They push open the heavy side door and step into a tiled entryway. A woman in navy overalls with short grey hair looks up from behind a counter.

'Can I help you?' she asks, ***friendly*** but clearly puzzled by the sight of three girls and one turquoise suitcase.

'Hi.' Ava steps forward. 'We're looking for someone who might've lost this suitcase?'

The firefighter looks perplexed. 'I'm sorry, what did you say?'

‘It’s a really long story,’ Jo says, ‘but we’ve lost my suitcase which looks just like *this* suitcase. *This* suitcase doesn’t belong to us and we’re trying to find the owner. Because we hope then we might get *my* suitcase back. We think she might be a former netball player . . . maybe part of the 2002 Commonwealth Games team?’

The firefighter takes in Jo’s story. ‘And why do you think she might be here?’

‘A fortune teller who goes by the name Seraphina told us to come here,’ cuts in Lila. ‘She mentioned big red doors and the ringing of bells, so we figured this must be the place.’

The firefighter laughs gently. 'Girls, is this some kind of prank?'

'No,' says Jo. 'She might've been here today? Or maybe . . . yesterday? She'd be older now. Like, a grown-up. Possibly famous?'

'Well, everyone who works here is a grown-up, although none of us are ***famous***. You might be in the wrong place.'

The girls deflate slightly.

'Thanks anyway,' says Jo. She turns toward the door, suitcase wheels bumping behind her.

Back on the street, Lila starts to laugh.

'I can't believe we just did that. The great Seraphina must

be laughing her head off right now.'

Ava joins in the laughter as Jo plonks down on the suitcase.

'At least this case is good for one thing,' Jo says.

Suddenly, the ***firefighter*** sticks her head out of a window on the first floor. 'Hey – you might be thinking of The Firehouse Cafe. It used to be the local firehouse before this one was built. It's just around the corner, on Little Market Lane.'

Ava spins. 'Wait – Seraphina was telling us about a *cafe*?'

'Thank you!' Jo grins and waves at the firefighter. 'You've been super helpful!'

52

They round the corner, the afternoon sun casting long shadows as a painted sign comes into view: *The Firehouse Cafe – Where every cup sparks a story.*

They step towards the red doors, the smell of coffee and toasted banana bread drifting out into the street.

'Okay,' says Jo, 'let's see if the great Seraphina really does have a gift.'

CHAPTER SIXTEEN

The Firehouse Cafe is busy. The girls step inside and hover ***awkwardly*** near the door. There's a hum of conversation competing with the roar of the coffee grinder.

Jo scans the room. 'What are we even looking for?'

'A fit-looking netball player in her forties?' says Ava, only half-joking.

Jo's gaze lands on a group of four women at a corner table. They're mid-forties, maybe older, all in activewear. Their cheeks are flushed, possibly from an intense **gossip** session, or they've just come from a game. One of them laughs so loudly it turns a few heads.

Jo sighs. This might be embarrassing, but there's only one way to find out if the suitcase's owner is here.

Before the others can stop her, she starts threading her way between tables.

'Excuse me,' she says, stopping in front of the women.

They all look up mid-sip. One of them lowers her flat white. Their conversation dies mid-sentence.

'Sorry to interrupt,' Jo says, her voice higher than usual. 'I'm trying to return this suitcase to its owner. It's not one of yours, by any chance?'

A long pause. Then a slow shake of the head from a woman with bobbed hair and a big smile.

'Sorry, love,' she says. 'We're all locals. None of us is missing a suitcase.'

Jo's face burns. 'Right, no worries. Just thought I'd ask . . .'

Another woman raises an eyebrow. 'Sounds intriguing. Good luck with the **mystery**.'

'Thanks,' Jo says quickly, retreating back through the cafe.

Ava raises her brows. 'Well?'

'Nope,' Jo mutters. 'Pretty sure they're talking about me right now.'

'They definitely are,' says Lila,

glancing over Jo's shoulder. 'But hey, what about *her*?'

She nods toward a woman in her early forties sitting with a younger woman – maybe her daughter – sharing a plate of chips and deep in conversation.

'Maybe she's here to visit her daughter.'

Jo backs up. 'Your turn.'

'Oh no,' Lila says, grinning. 'I'm just the emotional support. This is all you, Aves.'

Ava **groans** but steps forward. 'Fine. I'll take one for the team.'

She walks over just as the two women fall silent and look up, chips held mid-air.

'Hi,' Ava says, trying to sound casual. 'Sorry to bother you, but we're trying to track down the owner of this suitcase.'

She gestures to the case as if it's a ***prize*** they might win on a game show. Both women glance at the case, then shake their heads almost in unison.

'Nope,' the older woman says politely. 'Sorry.'

'No worries,' Ava says with a smile.

Ava grabs the case and marches back to Jo and Lila.

'Well?' Jo asks.

'No dice.'

Jo sighs. 'I'm starting to think Seraphina might have been conning us.'

'You *think*?' Lila deadpans.

'I mean, it'd be *wild* if she actually knew anything real about this suitcase,' Jo adds.

'Exactly,' says Ava. 'Crystal balls aren't exactly known for their **tracking** skills.'

'We should have asked her what was inside – that would have revealed her real gift!' Jo laughs.

'Come on, we better meet Mum and Aunty Claire before they think we've disappeared,' says Lila.

They start toward the door, weaving through the cafe, the suitcase still trailing behind them like a ball and chain.

That's when a young male waiter intercepts them, holding a tray stacked with dirty plates.

'Hey – sorry,' he says, lowering his voice. 'My name's Thomas. I couldn't help overhearing. I think I know the owner of that suitcase.'

CHAPTER SEVENTEEN

'And we're *looking* for the owner,' Jo says cautiously. 'Who is it?'

Thomas leans in a little. 'This is probably nothing, but just before you arrived, I had a big table of women for lunch. All in their forties, really **lively** bunch – kind of took over the back corner.'

'Okay . . .' says Ava.

‘Cut to the chase, Thomas.’ Lila’s eyes narrow.

Thomas nods toward the case. ‘One of them had a suitcase that looked *exactly* like that. Same colour, same size, everything.’

The girls **glance** at each other. Jo’s grip on the handle tightens.

‘Do you remember anything else?’ asks Ava.

Thomas thinks. ‘Not really. They left about ten minutes ago. I can check if they paid cash or card, maybe get a name?’

Jo straightens. ‘Yes, please.’

As Thomas disappears behind the counter, the three girls look at each other – half excited, half freaked out.

'This is getting weird,' Lila says.

'You think that *now* it's getting weird?' Ava deadpans.

'Yeah. And I have a feeling it's about to get weirder.'

A moment later, Thomas reappears, holding something small between his fingers. Jo watches him and realises she's holding her breath.

'They paid cash, so no help with a name, sorry.'

Ava ***groans***.

Thomas signals that he's not done talking. 'But when I cleared their table, this was stuck under one of the napkins.' He hands it to Jo. It's a slightly crumpled paper stub.

Jo frowns at it, then hands it to Ava. 'Okay. *Now* it's officially weird.'

'What is it?' Lila leans in.

'It's a ticket,' Ava says slowly. 'For the Southern Flames netball game. Tonight.'

Lila blinks. 'That *has* to be a coincidence. Yeah?'

'Seraphina was right!' Ava gasps. 'I mean – that's seriously **spooky**. I had her pegged as a total fraud.'

'She never asked us for money,' Jo points out. 'Maybe she actually *does* have a gift.'

Jo glances around the cafe, half expecting Seraphina to reappear through a beaded curtain. 'It's like we're in some kind of **cosmic mystery**.'

Lila checks her phone. 'I'll tell you what we are. Late!'

CHAPTER EIGHTEEN

Aunty Meg and Ava's mum are already waiting beside the car, standing in the shade and sipping iced coffees. As the girls pile into the back seat, the ***chatter*** begins almost immediately – the suitcase being taken, the fortune teller, the cafe and, of course, the ticket stub for a game they are headed to right now.

'My *goodness*, you girls have been busy,' Aunty Meg laughs as she signals right and merges into traffic.

'We just went for coffee and lost all of our savings trying to win an oversized stuffed toy,' Ava's mum adds with a grin. 'Clearly, we missed the *real* fun.'

'So, hang on,' says Ava, knees jiggling, 'there's actually a chance Jo's suitcase is at the stadium!'

Ava's mum turns to face the back seat. 'I wouldn't get your hopes up too high. There'll be thousands of people there tonight.'

Jo doesn't answer. Her stomach is doing Olympic-level ***flips*** at the thought of playing in front of that many people. She's been so caught up in chasing after the suitcase and trying to find its owner, she's managed to forget that she is about to play netball in front of the ***biggest crowd ever***.

Aunty Meg meets her eyes in the rear-view mirror. 'You've got this, girls. It's just like any other game.'

'Except,' Ava says, 'with a few thousand more eyeballs watching us.'

'*Aaaargh*,' Jo groans, dropping her head into her hands.

'Great pep talk, Mum,' Lila says, smirking.

Outside the car windows, the city is bustling – streets filled with fans in red and gold gear, some with faces painted, others waving homemade signs. As they turn a corner, the stadium looms into view. It's ***huge***, glowing and ***buzzing*** with noise like a living thing.

'There it is,' Ava says quietly.

Jo swallows. Her palms are clammy. The suitcase handle slips slightly in her grip. She's reminded of how tight the sneakers are and how it's not a case of whether she gets blisters, but of how many.

Ava's mum turns around in the front seat. 'You're going to be amazing.'

Jo tries to smile. 'Thanks.'

The car crawls up to the staff entrance. A woman in a headset stands by a temporary barrier, clipboard in hand. She waves them forward. As the car pulls to a halt, Aunty Meg leans out the window and gives their names.

'We'll be out there cheering you on,' says Ava's mum. 'Remember to breathe. And have ***fun***!'

Ava and Lila nod. Jo reaches for the door handle.

'Here we go,' she says, half to herself.

Jo steps out of the car, suitcase in hand and heart pounding as the stadium doors seem to rise higher and higher in front of her.

CHAPTER NINETEEN

If the stadium looks like a ***cool*** spaceship from the outside, it feels more like a rabbit warren on the inside.

'Wait for me!'

Jo trails after Ava and Lila through a maze of corridors, pulling her trusty suitcase sidekick behind her. Jo feels more nervous than she's ever felt before a game, but she also knows that nerves are important. It's been a very long day, but she ***suddenly*** feels super charged as they walk past catering staff, managers on two-way radios, coaches and, of course, players.

'That was Amanda Salmon,' Ava whispers to Jo, staring at the retreating figure of the legendary Wing Defence from the Southern Flames.

Jo feels herself nodding but she has no words.

A few corridors later, Jo recognises another hero. She slows her pace as her brain catches up.

Olivia Browne . . . all-star Centre legend.

It takes Jo a second to realise she's stopped moving. Lila is grinning at both of them.

'Looking a little starstruck, Country,' says Lila. 'Come on, we're nearly there.'

Lila enters a changing room and the girls follow. Inside, the atmosphere is ***charged*** with nerves. Even Perfect Plait looks pale. Ava and Jo smile nervously at the others. Lila grabs two team shirts and hands them one each.

Jo pulls on the purple shirt. At least it fits.

Jo splashes cold water on her face and checks her appearance in the bathroom mirror. She runs her fingers through her fringe and tightens her ponytail. She flexes her feet inside the sneakers, trying to find more room. She's almost got used to the blistered feeling between her toes. In an hour's time, she'll never have to wear these sneakers again.

Then they're all sitting around staring at each other. A few of the girls look ***quizzically*** at Jo's suitcase but nobody says anything. Everyone's too nervous to make conversation.

'Bayside Thunder Under Twelves!' cries a booming voice.

The arrival of Coach Bree brings a welcome burst of positive energy.

'The shirts look ***awesome***. Purple Thunder, here we come!'

Jo giggles.

Coach Bree takes them all in.

'Goodness me, you all look petrified.'

'I think I might be sick,' says one girl, who does look awfully green.

'No!' says Coach Bree. 'Remember, girls, we're here to have fun! If you're nervous about the crowd, just remember – they *love* the half-time games. They see you as the future of netball.'

All of a sudden, it's their time.

The glare of the stadium lights takes some getting used to. Jo, Ava and the rest of the team file into the seating area by the sideline, ready

to watch the professionals play the first half.

Jo feels her nerves shifting into something else: ***excitement***. From down here, she can see everything.

The crowd roars, big speaker music blares and the Southern Flames are giving it all they've got.

Jo can't look away. The passes, the speed, the defence – it's electric. Every move is ***sharp***. Every goal brings a new wave of noise.

Ava leans in. 'They make it look so easy.'

'Yeah,' Jo says, eyes locked on the game. 'Look at how fit they are.'

It's totally inspiring to watch. Jo cheers as Olivia Browne darts past a defender. She flicks a no-look pass to the Goal Attack, who sinks a shot from the edge of the circle. The crowd erupts. Her teammates crowd around her, shouting and hugging in celebration. Jo feels something shift inside her.

This is what she came for.

Coach Bree claps. 'All right, almost time!'

'Ready?' asks Ava.

'***Ready***!' says Jo. And she means it.

CHAPTER TWENTY

'Yoo-hoo!'

Jo turns to see a woman in the crowd waving. At first, she thinks it's Ava's mum or Aunty Meg, but she knows they're seated in the other stand.

'Wait for me!' cries the woman as she waves again.

Yes, it's as Jo thought. The woman is calling to *her*. But then Jo sees she's dragging something behind her. It's a turquoise suitcase that looks *exactly* like Jo's. The red ribbon tied to the handle is ***unmistakable***.

Jo spins around – there's the *other* suitcase still sitting next to Lila on the sidelines.

The woman waves again. 'You! I think we swapped bags!'

Jo's jaw drops.

'Am I happy to see you!' Jo waves to the woman, who makes her way down the stairs and joins Jo on the sidelines.

'You've got my suitcase?' says Jo. It's almost too good to be true.

'Yes, and I saw you arrive with mine,' says the woman. 'Your pass for the stadium was in your case, so I had a pretty good feeling you would be here tonight. A few phone calls confirmed you were playing at half-time.'

'It's here! My stuff!' Jo has unzipped the top of her suitcase and is rummaging through the bags of nuts. 'Mini Billie!' Jo pulls out the soft toy, ***delighting*** in her favourite plush puppy's slightly crumpled face. Jo hugs it tight.

'Yesss!' Ava laughs. 'Just in time. Change your sneakers! We've got a game to play!'

Jo doesn't need telling twice. She kicks off Lila's sneakers and laces up her own. The fit, the grip – *finally*. She wonders if everyone can hear her toes give a loud cry of ***relief***.

Lila has seen the woman with Jo's suitcase and walks over to them. She hands over the one she has been looking after. 'Are you like, super famous or something?' Lila asks her.

'Um . . .' Jo wants to chat to the woman who returned her suitcase but there isn't enough time before the game. 'How did you find us? Thank you! Are you really a medal winner?'

'I'll talk to you all afterwards,' the woman says, laughing. 'Go play!'

Jo hands mini Billie to Lila. 'Do. Not. Lose. Her.'

Lila nods, her expression serious. She's got the message.

Coach Bree calls them in.

'All right. This is your moment. I don't care if you win or lose – I care that you work together. Call for the ball. Support each other. ***Trust*** each other. Got it?'

The girls nod.

Jo looks around. Some teammates still look uncertain. A few fidget with their bibs.

She looks down at her GD bib and then steps into the centre of the circle.

'Hey. Quick thing before we run on. I know this morning felt rough.

But that was just one session. We've got one game now to show what we've got. It's okay to be ***nervous*** . . . I'm really nervous. But let's back each other. Let's make it fun. We've got this.'

There's a pause.

Then Ava nods. Even Perfect Plait gives a small nod and mutters, 'Yeah, what Jo said.'

Jo does a double take. 'You know my name?'

'Sure,' says Perfect Plait. 'And my name's Grace.'

Jo grins.

Together, they run onto the court.

Jo's heart thuds, but instead of nerves, she feels excited.

They're bouncing on their toes, waiting for the whistle. The half-time music blasts. The announcer's voice **echoes** through the speakers:

'Please welcome our first junior showcase team – the Bayside Thunder Under Twelves!'

CHAPTER TWENTY-ONE

Jo is in position. Her Goal Attack gives her a brief smile. She looks fit and fast.

'The Bayside Thunder Under Twelves will take on the West Coast Gazelles Under Twelves. Players on both teams have been specially selected from across the state to play here tonight.

What an honour for them and a treat for you!'

The whistle blows. Despite the noise from the crowd, Jo knows she has a job to do. She's not going to get distracted.

It's game on.

Ava ***explodes*** down the wing.

Lila's voice rings out from the sideline. 'Go, Ava! Go, go, go!'

Ava passes high and, suddenly, Jo has the ball.

Don't fumble now.

Jo plants her foot and looks around. The tall Goal Attack is on her and is blocking her line of sight, arms up, closing space. Jo pivots sharply on her grounded foot. She swings the ball around and fires it long to their Centre. She's fast with her pivot and ***perfectly*** calculates the move to Grace, who is charging into the goal circle. Grace catches the pass and shoots in one fluid movement.

Boom. First shot in. Goal.

There's a roar like thunder and it takes Jo a second to realise it's the

crowd cheering. Someone ***claps*** her on the back. A Gazelle even compliments her. 'Nice set-up.'

The girls grin at each other. Jo and Grace high-five, palms sweaty.

Oh my gosh, thinks Jo, *this feels amazing.*

She ***shadows*** the Goal Attack, a slippery mover who tries to feint wide, then cuts in. Jo sticks with her like glue, eyes sharp, feet light. Arms out, timing her jumps. The other team's Centre is slick, with fast hands and fast feet.

Lila calls out again. 'Watch the switch, Jo!'

Just then the Goal Attack tries to roll back. Jo is ready and reads the direction of the pass. Her hands just make contact and she grabs the ball. Jo sends it low, and all too soon it's back down the court.

Ava sprints, dragging her Wing Defence wide then doubling back to shake her. She catches clean, ***fakes*** a pass left, spins right – and it's another goal.

More cheers from the crowd. Jo can only make out a few words from the speakers as the game is commentated.

Jo scans the crowd for Aunty Meg and Ava's mum. There they are, halfway up the stands. Ava's mum is waving, both of them ***beaming*** like they've already won. Jo waves back and it gives her a new burst of energy.

Centre pass. Ava flicks to Jo – quick touch, then a fast bounce to Grace cutting through the middle.

Jo drops back again, ***defending*** with every ounce she's got. The Goal Attack tries another dodge, but Jo is quicker this time. She stays tight, times her leap and tips the ball again.

Lila's voice cuts through, 'Yes, Jo! You've got this!'

Jo's grinning now.

They move as one. Ava catches and swings it in fast. The shot goes up, but it misses.

Another Thunder player is already there, ***crashing*** into the circle. She grabs the rebound, twisting mid-air. Landing hard, she flicks it back.

Second shot – *goal.*

The crowd erupts.

Jo's heart lifts. It's not just excitement anymore, or nerves or feeling overwhelmed. She feels pure *joy*.

This is their moment. And Coach Bree was so right. Play well, have fun. Jo is so ***focused*** on her body and on the game that it's a surprise when the final whistle blows.

Jo stands still for a beat, sweat sticking her hair to her forehead. Her chest heaves.

She wasn't even keeping score during play, but a quick check of the board tells Jo that they **won** by four goals!

Even better! Jo thinks with delight.

Their team huddles, sharing breathless pats on the back and high-fives.

'You were amazing,' Ava says, slinging an arm around Jo's shoulders.

Jo grins. 'You, too.'

Jo looks up at the stands. So many people are cheering for them. It makes her feel **dizzy**.

Coach Bree steps up, clapping. 'That,' she says, 'was a brilliant team effort. You should be proud.'

Lila joins them, her face glowing. 'You guys smashed it!' She hands mini Billie to Jo. 'I can't cope with the responsibility. Mini Billie is officially back in your care.'

Jo happily accepts her pup. She breathes in her smell. She smells like all the ***good*** things in the world: she smells like home.

As they walk off the court, Jo catches sight of the woman with the turquoise suitcase waiting for them just beyond the gate.

CHAPTER TWENTY-TWO

Aunty Meg nudges Jo. 'Is that her?'

'Yes,' Jo replies.

They watch as two young girls ask the woman for an autograph. And, just like that, Jo is filled with nerves again. Jo remembers the ***gold medal*** in the woman's suitcase. Whoever she is, she's a living netball legend and *she* just watched *them* play.

Ava and Lila fall in beside Jo as they weave their way around the crowd to reach the woman. Ava's mum and Aunty Meg hang back, giving them space but watching on. They find a space away from the crowds between a coffee cart and an ice-cream vendor.

Ava breaks the silence with an awkward ***outburst***. 'We saw your medal in your suitcase! You're a pro netballer, right?'

The woman chuckles. 'I'm Nicola Foster, Commonwealth Games 2002, Manchester. Goalkeeper. One wonky knee and a gold medal to show for it.'

'No *way*,' Lila breathes.

'Way,' Nicola grins. 'I'm in town for a reunion with the rest of the squad. We try to catch up every few years.'

Jo stares. 'That's . . . wow.'

'*You* girls are wow. You played like you meant it out there,' Nicola says. '***Tight*** defence, ***smart*** passes.'

Jo shrugs, flustered. 'Thanks.'

Ava opens her mouth, but no words come out.

'You don't have to be the flashiest or the fastest to be great – you just need to back each other. That's what wins games. That's what makes it fun.'

Jo nods, gripping mini Billie a little tighter to her chest.

'Besides,' Nicola adds, 'you're miles ahead of where I was at your age. Keep showing up like you did today, and who knows? Maybe I'll be the one asking *you* for ***autographs***.'

Ava glances at Jo, then Lila. 'Um . . . would it be weird if we asked *you* for one now?'

Nicola laughs. 'Tell you what, I'll do you one better. Want a photo?'

'Yes, please,' the girls say in unison, signalling to some of their team to join in.

Jo feels like pinching herself. This must be a dream.

Aunty Meg steps in with her phone at the ready. 'I've got it – everyone squeeze in.'

They bunch together, cheeks flushed, still ***buzzing*** from the game and from a chance meeting with a legend they will remember forever. Aunty Meg snaps the photo.

'Thanks,' Jo says, breathless.

Nicola nods. 'You're welcome. Keep going. Keep playing. And thanks for looking after my suitcase! As you can imagine, my

Commonwealth medal is extremely valuable to me.'

'It's very gold,' breathes Ava, still looking starstruck.

'It is!' Nicola laughs. 'It's important to me because it reminds me of a game that we thought we wouldn't win and yet, somehow, we did. We came together in a really **special** way. The medal reminds me of that feeling.'

'That's so cool,' says Jo.

'See you, girls,' says Nicola. With a last wave, Nicola turns and disappears into the crowd, her rightful suitcase rumbling behind her.

The girls stare after her for a second.

Then Lila says, 'Okay, but *that* was kind of epic, right?'

Ava nods. '**So epic**.'

Jo doesn't say anything. She just smiles. She gives mini Billie another squeeze.

'*That* was nuts.'

Coach Bree jogs past and gives them a smile. 'Follow me, girls. The Southern Flames would like to meet each of you after the game and were hoping for some photos.'

'Photos?' says Jo. 'Did Coach just say photos with the Southern Flames?'

'She did.' Lila motions for them to hurry after Coach.

Jo pauses. She's holding mini Billie under one arm and she has her suitcase in her other hand.

'Would one of you look after my suitcase for me?' Jo asks the group.

Jo is met with a resounding, '*No!*'

'All right, all right,' says Jo. 'Come on, old friend,' she mutters to the suitcase, giving it a tug. 'Turns out we're a package deal, but we're also kind of a *big* deal.'

Jo hurries to catch up to Ava and Coach Bree. It's been a ***wild ride*** in the city, but she'll soon be heading home with her own suitcase and some unforgettable memories.

CHAPTER TWENTY-THREE

The main station in Melbourne is busy and loud but, this time, Jo doesn't feel overwhelmed. She wheels her turquoise suitcase along the platform, mini Billie tucked safely under her arm.

Ava is beside Jo, ***chattering*** non-stop.

'I can't wait to give the club our presentation. And show them the photo of us with Nicola!'

'We can write some of it on the train,' Jo suggests. 'It'll give you something to do.'

Ava grins and turns her head. 'Come on, Mum!'

Ava's mum is a few steps behind them. She's carrying a small white box tied with blue string.

They reach their carriage. The familiar silver train waits, ***humming*** and ***gleaming*** in the afternoon sun.

They stow their bags, and Jo feels a surge of happiness when her suitcase slots perfectly into the luggage rack. No more lost luggage. No more drama.

'Window seat again?' Ava asks.

'Your turn.' Jo waits while Ava slides across the row of seats to the window. Jo takes the middle seat, with mini Billie ***snuggly*** nestled on her lap.

Jo finds it hard to believe she's heading home already. In one way it feels as if she's been gone for ages but, in another, her city adventure happened way too quickly.

The whistle blows. The train jolts into motion and the city starts to slowly slide away behind them.

'Aunty Meg and I made a quick stop at Ava's favourite bakery,'

Ava's mum says, handing the box to Jo. 'A little something for the trip home.'

Jo lifts the lid and grins. Six ***doughnuts***, golden and dusted in sugar, still warm.

'Way to go, Mum!' Ava grabs a doughnut.

'Thank you!' Jo says. 'You're the best.'

Ava unwraps a doughnut and takes a huge bite. 'Mmmmmm,' she says around a mouthful. 'Best. Trip. Ever.'

Jo laughs, taking a smaller, neater bite of her own doughnut. 'Agreed.'

Ava's mum smiles over her book.

Jo leans back in her seat. She looks forward to the scenery changing from ***cityscape*** to ***countryside*** – walnut orchards, open paddocks, distant hills. Home.

Ava dusts sugar off her tracksuit pants. 'When we get back, your cows better not have escaped.'

'Billie's in charge,' Jo says, grinning. 'And if all else fails, she'll bribe them with nuts.'

Ava snorts. 'That's your whole family's solution for **everything**. Lost cows? Nuts. Lost suitcase? Nuts. Nervous about the game? Definitely nuts.'

Jo laughs so hard, she nearly chokes on a bite of doughnut. 'Good thing I'm *nut* crazy!'

They settle back, shoulders bumping playfully.

Ava nudges her. 'Want a game?' she asks, waving a battered UNO pack.

Jo grins. 'You're on.'

As they shuffle the cards and stuff their mouths full of doughnuts,

Jo looks out at the wide, open fields blurring past.

The city has been ***incredible***.

But right now, heading home with her best friend, mini Billie, a box of doughnuts and a million new memories, Jo wouldn't trade this moment for anything.

Look out for more adventures
with ***Jo***, ***Ava*** and ***Billie*** –
– coming soon!

ABOUT JO WESTON

Jo Weston grew up on her parents' nut farm in rural Victoria. She moved to Melbourne at age six and soon after joined the Waverley Netball Club, where her love of netball began. Jo is now a senior member of both the Melbourne Vixens and Australian Diamonds.

As one of Australia's best defenders, Jo helped lead the Diamonds to gold at the 2022 Commonwealth Games and the 2023 World Cup. With the Melbourne Vixens Jo was instrumental in the team's Premiership win in 2020 and Minor Premiership of 2022.

Away from the court, Jo is passionate about environmental causes, her beloved Essendon FC and her Australian Shepherd, Billie.